Through Tsavo

A Story of an East African Savanna

The
Nature
Conservancy®

*Dedicated to my "core group" at Trinity,
and my parents — for believing I could
do anything and for teaching me
how to use my strengths. —S.B.*

For my sons, Joel and Marshall. —P.K.

Illustrations copyright © 1998 Paul Kratter.
Book copyright © 1998 Trudy Corporation, 353 Main Avenue, Norwalk, CT 06851.

Soundprints is a division of Trudy Corporation, Norwalk, Connecticut.

Book layout: Diane Hinze Kanzler
Editor: Judy Gitenstein

First Edition 1998
10 9 8 7 6 5 4 3 2
Printed in Hong Kong

Acknowledgments:
   Our very special thanks to Michael Devlin of the Endangered Wildlife Trust
for his review and guidance.
   Thanks to Mike, for your time and enthusiasm. Without your help, this could
not have happened. —S.B.
   Thank you to the staff at the Oakland Zoo. —P.K.

Library of Congress Cataloging-in-Publication Data

Bull, Schuyler

Through Tsavo: a story of an East African savanna / by Schuyler Bull ;
illustrated by Paul Kratter.
          p.   cm.
Summary: Follows a herd of elephants, including a playful young calf, as it slowly
makes its way in Tsavo National Park in Kenya to the Mzima River during a long,
dry season.
          ISBN 1-56899-552-0 (hardcover)   ISBN 1-56899-553-9 (pbk.)
1. African elephant — Kenya — Tsavo National Park — Juvenile literature.
[1. African elephant. 2. Tsavo National Park (Kenya). 3. Elephants.]
I. Kratter, Paul, ill. II. Title.
          QL737.P98B85 1998   97-47611
          599.67'4'0967623 — dc21   CIP
                                                                AC

Through Tsavo

A Story of an East African Savanna

by Schuyler Bull
Illustrated by Paul Kratter

Soundprints
Where Children Discover...

It is near the end of a long, dry season in Tsavo National Park in Kenya, Africa. A bolt of lightning zips down the sky, starting a fire in the parched, golden grass. The matriarch, or female head of an elephant family, sniffs the breeze, keeping her calf close by.

It has not rained for weeks and the elephants are traveling to the mouth of the Mzima River in search of water. The herd has passed other small fires, which burn away the brush and leaves, but die out before hurting the larger trees. The smoke in the air makes Elephant Calf sneeze.

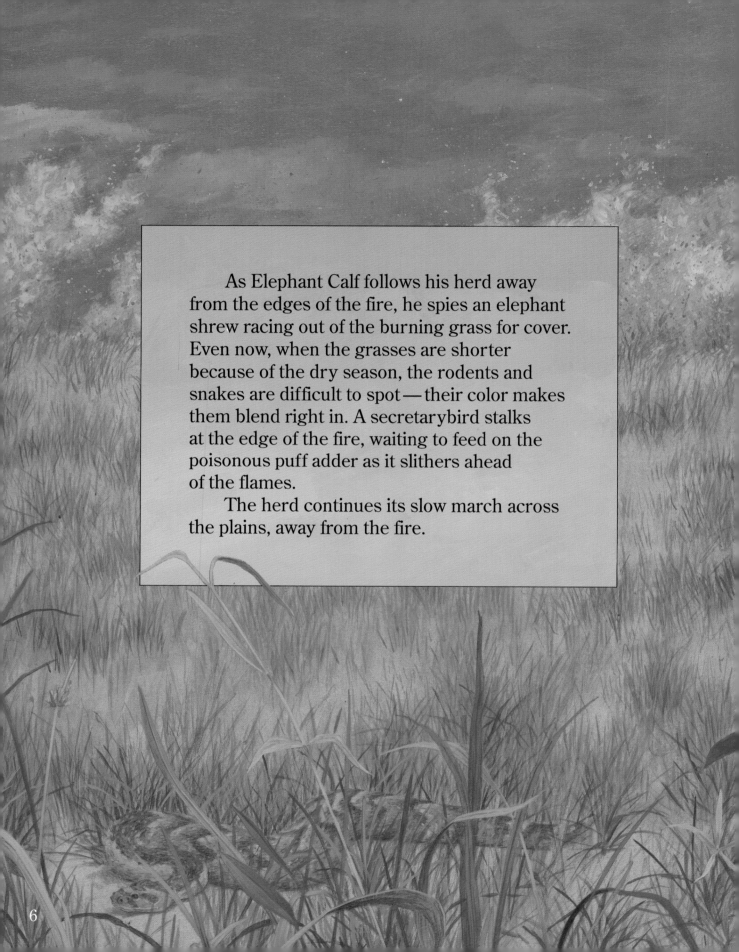

As Elephant Calf follows his herd away
from the edges of the fire, he spies an elephant
shrew racing out of the burning grass for cover.
Even now, when the grasses are shorter
because of the dry season, the rodents and
snakes are difficult to spot—their color makes
them blend right in. A secretarybird stalks
at the edge of the fire, waiting to feed on the
poisonous puff adder as it slithers ahead
of the flames.

The herd continues its slow march across
the plains, away from the fire.

Elephant Calf can't resist using his trunk to explore a huge, chimney-shaped termite mound as the herd stops for a rest. A colony of dwarf mongoose have adopted the mound as a home. Deep in the mound, a termite frog lies buried, waiting for the rains to begin.

Elephant Calf wriggles his trunk into a hole, but the hole is too small and he cannot reach very far down. A snort from his mother sends him trotting back to her side as the herd continues along the savanna.

From its perch, a hungry black-shouldered kite watches for escaping termites.

At midday, the elephant herd stops to rest in a small acacia grove. While the others doze, Elephant Calf's mother peels off long ribbons of bark, stuffing a few in her mouth with her trunk.

Elephant Calf plays with the hanging strips and sets them swinging. Then, catching one strip between his teeth, he pulls the bark down with his weight. His mother raises one leg and lets out a soft rumble, telling the herd that it is time to move on.

They begin moving again. Cattle egrets ride on the backs of the elephants, keeping a sharp lookout for insects or frogs unearthed along the way. They also search the elephants for ticks and scabs. Elephant Calf feels the scratch of their beaks on his skin.

Elephant Calf notices a black-throated honeyguide leading a honey badger to a beehive with a flick of its white tail feathers. After the badger claws open the hive and begins eating, the honeyguide joins in to eat wax, bee larvae, and eggs.

13

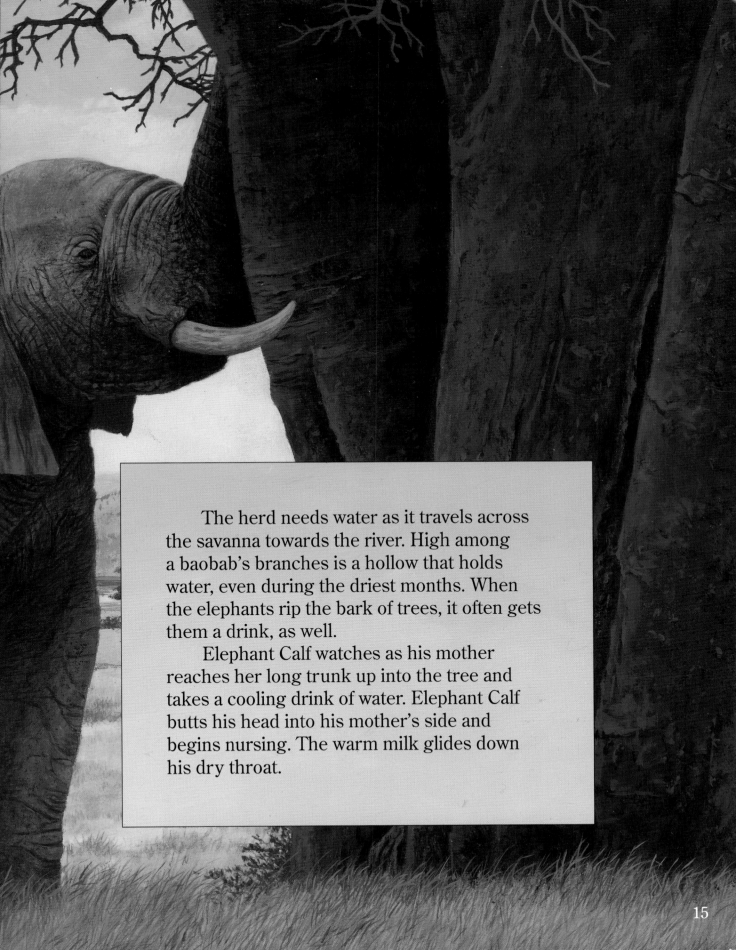

The herd needs water as it travels across the savanna towards the river. High among a baobab's branches is a hollow that holds water, even during the driest months. When the elephants rip the bark of trees, it often gets them a drink, as well.

Elephant Calf watches as his mother reaches her long trunk up into the tree and takes a cooling drink of water. Elephant Calf butts his head into his mother's side and begins nursing. The warm milk glides down his dry throat.

Once finished drinking, the herd moves onward. When his mother suddenly changes direction, Elephant Calf looks up. A short distance away, he sees vultures circling down from their roosts in a tree. Below, hunched over its dinner, a cheetah tries to fend off a pack of hyenas. As the hyenas circle closer and closer, the cheetah is finally forced to give up its dinner and slink away. The hyenas are soon joined by the vultures as they finish off the cheetah's meal.

The elephant herd stays clear and moves on.

Dust raised by the herd's feet swirls onto a group of giraffes, feeding among the branches of umbrella-shaped acacia trees. Elephant Calf stares at their long necks and colorful coats as they pass. The giraffes eat mouthfuls of leaves at a time. The acacia's three-inch thorns are no match for their eighteen-inch tongues.

The adult elephants are paying special attention to some black-maned lions in the distance. Since there is no cause for alarm, they continue to forage for leaves, grass, fruit, and bark. Some vulturine guinea fowl race ahead of the elephants' giant feet.

Elephant Calf follows a dung beetle that is rolling a piece of elephant dropping in a ping-pong-sized ball. The beetle pushes the ball to her underground tunnel. Later she and her mate will lay their eggs in the dung and raise their brood in the tunnel.

The herd has moved ahead. Suddenly, Elephant Calf hears a warning trumpet from his mother — he has lagged too far behind for safety. A large crocodile hiding in the shade under a bush would snap up an elephant calf if given the chance. He trots back to his mother's side.

Finally, the elephant herd reaches the clear pools at the mouth of the Mzima. Swimming hippos, turtles, and fish can be seen from the bank. Cape buffalo, black rhino, and the lesser kudu stand in small clusters at the muddy edges. The elephants splash into the water, drinking in long, slurpy sips.

A Nile crocodile on the far bank basks in the hot afternoon sun. Elephant Calf's mother keeps a wary eye out, ready to attack if it comes too close.

Elephant Calf kneels down to play and roll in the cooling mud at the edges of the pools. He covers himself with the soothing mud. It will protect him from the sun, as well as from biting insects.

In a tall, scraggly baobab tree that shades an end of the pool, a red-billed buffalo weaver builds its untidy nest of sticks. Zebras come to graze in the long grass. A wildebeest and a dainty gazelle come to the waterhole, eating the shorter grasses.

Elephant Calf splashes all the way into the pool, licking at the water once or twice. It won't be long before the rainy season will begin, turning the savanna a lush green.

The sun is lowering, easing its heat on the savanna. Elephant Calf sprays himself with water from his trunk.

Two rock hyraxes absorb the last warmth from the sun-baked rocks. A yellow-billed hornbill cracks a seedcase with its strong bill. A pygmy falcon perches on an acacia branch, scanning the ground for prey.

As sunset turns the sky to fire, the elephant family forms a protective circle around Elephant Calf. With their tails to the outside, they will guard him against any dangers of the night.

Elephant Calf's mother nuzzles him with her trunk. He nestles into the dry grass and drifts off to sleep. The herd has found a place with plenty of food and water where they can stay, for now.

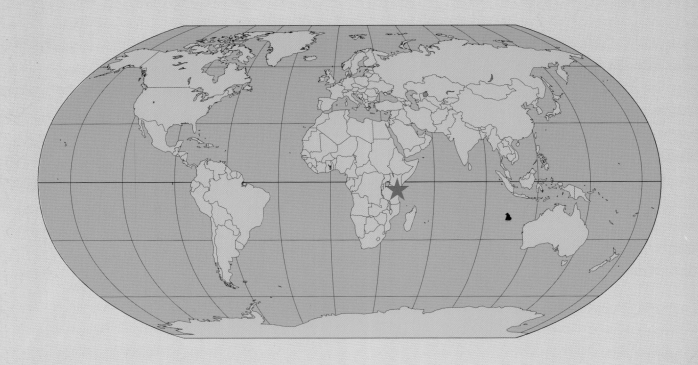

Tsavo National Park, Kenya, East Africa

Tsavo National Park is located in the south-eastern corner of Kenya, East Africa, bordering on Tanzania. It was declared a protected area in 1947.

About Tsavo

Tsavo National Park was made into a protected area in 1947. Before then, Tsavo was a *nyika thornveld* — mostly trees and shrubs with very little grass or open land. It was home to about 12,000–15,000 elephants. For generations the Wata, a native people living in this area, had hunted and killed about 400 elephants a year.

When Tsavo became a national park, no hunting of wild animals — by the Wata or any other people — was allowed inside the park boundaries. Without the Wata to control population, the number of elephants in the area quickly got bigger. They were joined by other herds of elephants who had been pushed out because of new settlements outside of Tsavo. The now huge elephant population destroyed the bush by breaking down underbrush and uprooting trees. Sunlight could now reach the ground, making grasses sprout and grow up over large stretches. This attracted new kinds of grass-eating mammals and field birds to come.

Then, in the 1970s, several years of drought turned Tsavo into a desert-like wasteland. Elephants died of starvation at alarming rates. When the drought finally ended, the landscape of Tsavo had changed. What was once *nyika thornveld* had become a grassland, or savanna, with typical grazing animals, such as zebra and wildebeest.

Today, the number of elephants has balanced itself. Areas of grassland will get a little smaller as trees and shrubs begin to grow back in Tsavo's forests. But the savanna will probably go on being a good home for the many plants, birds, and mammals that moved in over the past fifty years. In the end, nature found a new balance for all the many species, plant and animal, that live inside the protective boundaries of Tsavo. The Wata people, however, had their way of life changed forever.

Glossary

▲ *Acacia Tree*

▲ *Eastern White-bearded Wildebeest*

▲ *Nile Crocodile*

▲ *African Elephant*

▲ *Gerenuk*

▲ *Plains Zebra*

▲ *Black Rhinoceros*

▲ *Giraffe*

▲ *Secretarybird*

▲ *Cape Buffalo*

▲ *Lesser Kudu*

▲ *Thomson's Gazelle*

▲ *African Pygmy Falcon*

▲ *Eastern Yellow-billed Hornbill*

▲ *Rock Hyrax*

▲ *Baobab Tree*

▲ *Hippopotamus*

▲ *Spotted Hyena*

▲ *Black-throated Honeyguide*

▲ *Honey Badger*

▲ *Vultures*

▲ *Cheetah*

▲ *Lion*

▲ *Vulturine Guineafowl*

▲ *Dwarf Mongoose*

▲ *White-headed Buffalo-weaver*